MYSTERY of the RUNAWAY SLED

Written by Erica Frost

Illustrated by Leigh Grant

Troll Associates

Troll Associates, Mahwah, N.J.

Library of Congress Catalog Card Number: 78-60124

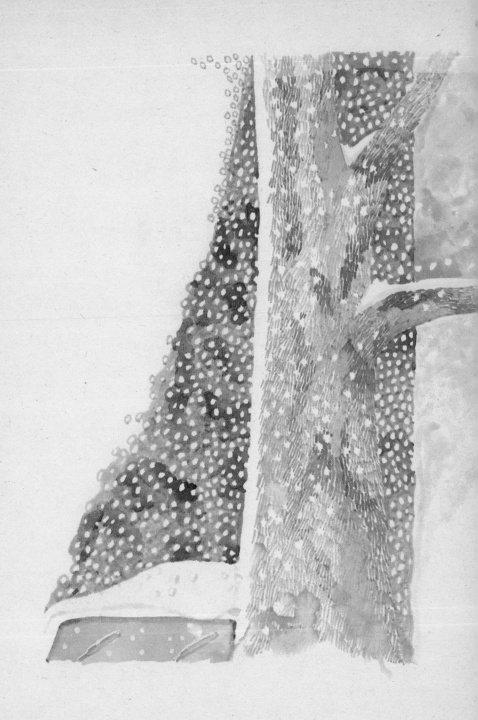

"Oh, boy!" said Rosie. "It's snowing!"
Soft white flakes were tumbling down.
Rosie watched them fall. They fell on trees
and lampposts. They made little pillows on
branches and cars.

It was dark outside. The snowflakes swirled and twirled. They looked like feathers, under the street lamp. They piled up, up, up.

That night, Rosie made a wish. "I wish it would snow all night," she whispered. Then she went to sleep and dreamed she was zooming down Piney Hill on her new sled.

The next morning, she ran to the
window. The snow was still there.
Everything was white.

"Oh, snow! I love you so!" she sang, as she washed her face.

"Oh, shnow! I ruv you sho!" she sang, as she brushed her teeth.

"It snowed!" she shouted as she ran down the stairs. "It snowed!"

"Thanks for telling me," said her brother Ralph. "I thought all that white stuff was ice cream!"

"Funny," said Rosie. "Very funny."

She phoned Willie. Willie had been her best friend ever since nursery school, when she had saved his chocolate cupcake from a giant spider.

"Come on over," said Rosie, "and bring your sled. We can go sledding on Piney Hill."

"Okay," said Willie. "I'll be there in an hour."

When Willie arrived, Rosie was ready and waiting.

"Snow, here I come!" said Rosie. "Come on, Willie. My sled is in the garage."

"I don't see it," said Willie.

"It was right here," said Rosie.

"Where?" asked Willie.

"It was behind the lawn mower," said Rosie. "I know it was. I saw it yesterday. I saw it with my own eyes."

"Well, it's not here today," said Willie. "Maybe somebody snitched it."

"Rats!" said Rosie. "Everything happens to me."

"Don't worry," said Willie. "We'll find it."

"Sure," said Rosie. "But where?"

Willie scratched his head. "I don't know," he said. "I haven't a clue."

"That's it!" cried Rosie. "We'll look for a clue. We'll track down the snitcher and make him give back my sled, or my name isn't Rosie Rooney!"

Rosie looked around. "Look here, Willie!" she called. "Footprints! There are footprints in the snow!"

"There are sled tracks, too!" cried Willie. "They go from your garage to Piney Hill. Whoever took your sled went that way."

They followed the footprints to Piney Hill.

"There's nobody here," said Willie.

"The trail goes up the hill," said Rosie. "Come on! Hurry up!"

They climbed the hill, side by side,
dragging Willie's sled behind them.

"We should act like real detectives," said Willie. "We should have code words and ask important questions."

"Okay," said Rosie. "Ask me a question."

"Ahem," said Willie. He cleared his throat. "Do you have any enemies, Miss Rooney?"

"Of course not," said Rosie. "I haven't an enemy in the world. Everyone loves me."

Willie tried again. "Tell me about your sled," he said. "What does it look like? I mean, is there anything special about your sled?"

"It's just a sled," said Rosie. "It's just a regular sled with my initials painted on it."

"Aha!" said Willie. "That's a clue. We now know that the missing sled has your initials painted on it!"

"Big deal," said Rosie. "I just said that."

"Well, what about the code?" asked

Willie. "I think we should have a code."

"All right," said Rosie. "If everything is okay, we yell *Yako!* That's okay spelled backwards. If there is trouble, we yell *Pleh!*"

"Agreed!" said Willie.

They came to the top of the hill.
Children were everywhere. They were
building snowmen. They were building
snow forts. They were having snowball
fights. There were sled tracks and footprints in every direction.

"Oh, no!" cried Willie. "What do we do now?"

"We cry," said Rosie.

"Hey!" said Willie. "Isn't that Marylou Higgins?"

"Hush your mouth!" said Rosie. "Don't ever say that name in front of me again!"

"Why not?" asked Willie. "Don't you like her?"

"Like her!" yelled Rosie. "That girl took my best idea for the science fair, and won first prize! She took a bite of my meat loaf sandwich when I wasn't looking! She took my spelling book, and didn't give it back until after the test! I wouldn't be a bit surprised if she took my sled, too!"

"Let's find out," said Willie.

Marylou Higgins was sitting on a new sled. She was wearing sunglasses and a hat with six pompoms.

"Nice sled you have there," said Rosie.

"You can't borrow it," said Marylou.

"I don't want to borrow it," said Rosie.

"I just want to see if certain initials are
painted on it."

"Get lost!" said Marylou.

Rosie reached over, and pulled Marylou's sunglasses off her nose. She put them
on.

"Give them back!" screeched Marylou.

"Make me!" said Rosie.

Marylou jumped up. She ran after Rosie. Willie kneeled down and looked at the sled. He looked for Rosie's initials. They were not there.

"Yako!" he yelled. "Yako! Yako!"
Rosie gave the sunglasses to Marylou.
"Here," she said. "Who wants your old
sunglasses, anyway?"

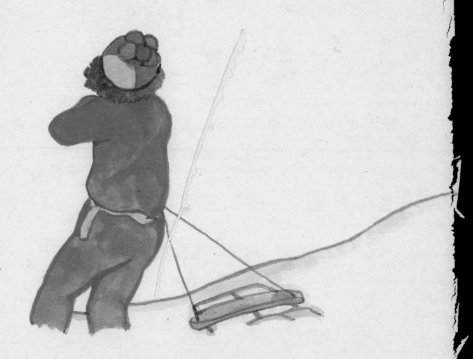

"I thought you didn't have an enemy in the world," said Willie. "What do you call Marylou?"

"I call her a rotten friend," said Rosie. "That's what I call her."

"Let's split up," said Willie. "You look here. I'll look over there."

"Okay," said Rosie. "Holler if you want me."

Willie clumped through the snow. He looked and looked. He looked everywhere for a sled with Rosie's initials.

Then he saw one. It was brand new.
Painted on it, in big, black letters, were the
initials R.R.

"Rosie Rooney!" said Willie. He picked
up the sled.

"Hey!" said a small voice. "Put that sled
down. It's mine."

"It is *not* your sled," said Willie. "This sled belongs to Rosie Rooney. Those are her initials."

"They are *my* initials," said the little boy. "I'm Robert Richards."

"Hah!" said Willie. "Do you expect me to believe that?"

"You can ask my big brother, if you don't believe me," said Robert Richards. "Here he is now."

Willie looked up. He looked up and up and up. A boy as big as an apartment house was standing next to Robert.

"What's the matter, Robbie?" he asked. "Is this cluck bothering you?"

"He took my sled," said Robert Richards. "He says it isn't mine."

"Oh, he did, did he?" said the giant.

"I only thought . . ." said Willie.

"Don't think!" said Robert's big brother.

"Pleh!" hollered Willie. "Pleh! Pleh!"

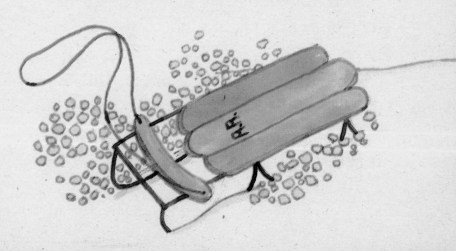

"It's no use," said Rosie. "We'll never find it here. Let's go back to my garage. There may be a clue that we missed."

"Okay," said Willie. He sat down on his sled. "You pull me halfway. Then I'll pull you."

"I wonder who made those footprints," said Rosie.

"If we knew that," said Willie, "we would know everything."

"There must be a clue someplace," said Rosie.

They searched the garage carefully.

"Look!" cried Willie. "Take a look at these!"

He held up a pair of brown boots. They were covered with melting snow. Someone had worn them, not long ago.

Rosie took one boot. Willie took the other. They placed the boots in the snowy footprints.

"A perfect fit!" cried Willie.

"And I know who they belong to," said Rosie. "Come on, Willie! Follow me!"

"Okay!" said Rosie. She shook the wet boots under her brother's nose. "I know these are your boots! Don't deny it!"

"I don't deny it," said Ralph.

"So!" said Rosie. "You admit it! You admit that you snitched my sled!"

"I didn't snitch it," said Ralph. "I borrowed it. Don't be angry. I brought it back, didn't I?"

"No," said Rosie. "You didn't. It is not in the garage where it belongs."

"It's not?" said Ralph.

"It's not!" said Rosie.

"I just remembered," said Ralph. "I left it in front of the house. Really. Don't worry. It will still be there."

"It better be," said Rosie. "Come on, Willie! We're coming to the end of the trail!"

They looked, but the sled was nowhere in sight. Some children were building a snowman. A snow plow was coming down the street. That was all. There was no sled.

"Now it's really lost," said Rosie. "What am I going to do?" She sat down on a pile of snow. "I think my sled just ran away," she said.

"Don't be silly," said Willie. "Sleds don't run away."

"Then where is it?" asked Rosie. "Answer me that. Where is it?"

The snow plow came closer.

"Watch where you're going!" yelled one of the children. "You'll bury our snowman!"

"That's dumb," said Willie. "The plow came down this street before. There isn't enough snow on the street to bury their snowman."

"Willie!" yelled Rosie.

"Rosie!" yelled Willie.

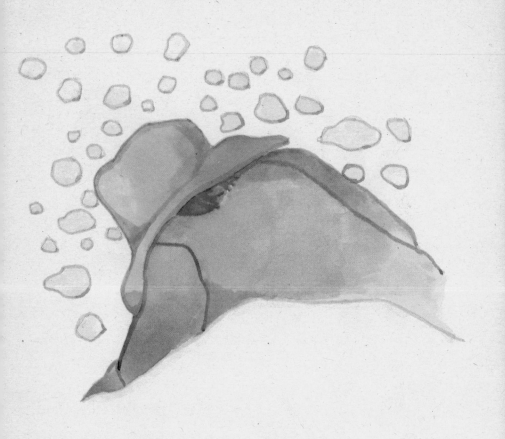

They jumped up, and began to dig in the snow.

"Yako!" yelled Willie, as he uncovered a runner.

"Yako!" yelled Rosie, as the rest of her sled appeared.

"Come on!" shouted Willie. "I'll race
you to Piney Hill!"

"Here I come!" shouted Rosie. "Here I
come!"